Twinkles, Arthur and Puss

Judith Kerr

HarperCollins *Children's Books*

Twinkles, Arthur and Puss

For my darling Tom

Picture books by Judith Kerr:

The Tiger Who Came to Tea

Mog the Forgetful Cat

Mog's Christmas

Mog and the Baby

Mog in the Dark

Mog's Amazing Birthday Caper

Mog and Bunny

Mog and Barnaby

Mog on Fox Night

Mog and the Granny

Mog and the V.E.T

Mog's Bad Thing

Goodbye Mog

How Mrs Monkey Missed the Ark

Birdie Halleluyah!

The Other Goose

Goose in a Hole

First published in Great Britain by HarperCollins Children's Books in 2007

1 3 5 7 9 10 8 6 4 2
ISBN-13: 978-0-00-725446-0
ISBN-10: 0-00-725446-6

HarperCollins Children's Books is a division of HarperCollins Publishers Ltd.
Text and illustrations copyright © Kerr-Kneale Productions Ltd 2007
The author/illustrator asserts the moral right to be identified as the author/illustrator of the work.
A CIP catalogue record for this title is available from the British Library.
Visit our website at: www.harpercollinschildrensbooks.co.uk

Printed and bound in Singapore

This is Grandpa.
He has a black cat. It is called Puss.

Puss has been Grandpa's
cat ever since she
was a kitten.

They like each other.

Sometimes
they do things
together.

They always have supper together and Grandpa cooks the same thing for them both. Grandpa is very fond of bacon and chips. Puss likes them sometimes.

This is the Jones family. They also have a black cat.
It walked in with the milkman one day looking very hungry.
So Mrs Jones gave it some cat food, and now it eats
a tin of cat food every morning for breakfast
and the children have called it Twinkles.

This is Lady Daisy.
She found a black cat outside
her window one day, looking very sad.
So she gave it some fish
and called it Arthur,

and now Arthur eats fish
for his lunch every day
and all Lady Daisy's friends
admire him.

Twinkles has a basket to sleep in.

Arthur has three cushions

and Puss sleeps on Grandpa's bed.
But day and night, Twinkles,
Arthur and Puss are out a lot,
and nobody knows where they go.

Grandpa thinks Puss
goes to play in the park.

Lady Daisy thinks Arthur goes to see his friends,

and the Jones children think that Twinkles
turns into SuperCat and has lots of adventures.

But they are all wrong.

And one day, Twinkles, Arthur and Puss all disappeared.

Twinkles didn't come to eat her breakfast,

Arthur didn't come
to eat his lunch,

and Puss didn't come to eat her supper.
This made Grandpa so sad that he
couldn't eat his supper either.

So that night Grandpa,

and Lady Daisy,

and all the Jones's went out in the dark
to look for their missing cats.

When it started to rain they all met under a big tree.

"I'm looking for my cat," said Grandpa.
"So am I," said Lady Daisy.
"And so are we," said the Jones's.

SUDDENLY
they heard a meow.

"It's Arthur!" shouted Lady Daisy.

"It's Twinkles!" shouted all the Jones's.

"No" said Grandpa. "It's Puss. It's my cat.
"Oh Puss, I'm so glad I've found you,"

"Puss?" said Lady Daisy. "*Your* cat? But I thought this was *my* cat and I call it Arthur!"

"Well, *we* call it Twinkles," cried all the Jones's.

"Puss," said Grandpa. "Whatever have you been up to?"

"This cat eats breakfast at our house
every day," said Mrs Jones.
"And I always give it lunch,"
said Lady Daisy.
"Oh dear," said Grandpa, "Puss, you have been a greedyguts."

The Jones children all began to cry.
They cried, "Twinkles!
We want Twinkles!"

Lady Daisy nearly cried too, she was so sad.
She said, 'Oh Arthur, whatever will I do without you?'
But then, suddenly, they heard…

a very small meow…

and another…

and another…

and another.

They were very small meows
because they were made
by very small cats.

"Kittens!" shouted Grandpa. "Puss, you old cleverclogs, you've had kittens!"

"Oh Arthur," said Lady Daisy. "I never thought that one day you'd become a mummy!"

"Can we have a kitten?" shouted the Jones children. "Please, please, please can we have a kitten?"

"Well, what do you think, Puss?" said Grandpa.
"We haven't got room for them all in our house."

So when the kittens were big enough
one went to live with Lady Daisy and
she called it Arthur and fed it on fish
and all her friends admired it.

And Arthur didn't miss his mummy
because she came to see him every day.
Usually at lunch time.

The other three kittens went to live with the Jones's and the children called them Twinkles, Tiddles and Twiddles and they each ate a tin of cat food every morning.

And they didn't miss their mummy either because
she came to see them every day at breakfast time.

But on Sundays they all went round
to Grandpa's house for a lovely big
supper of bacon and chips.

I am a greedyguts!